# The ABC Mystery

Story and Pictures by
**Doug Cushman**

HarperCollins*Publishers*

Reprinted by arrangement with
HarperCollins Publishers.
10  9  8  7  6  5  4  3  2

Library of Congress Cataloging-in-Publication Data
Cushman, Doug.
   The ABC mystery / story and pictures by Doug Cushman.
      p.     cm.
   Summary: An alphabetical list of people, objects, and clues leads Inspector
McGroom to a stolen work of art.
   ISBN 0-06-021226-8. — ISBN 0-06-021227-6 (lib. bdg.)
   ISBN 0-06-443459-1 (pbk.)
   [1. Mystery and detective stories.   2. Alphabet.   3. Stories in rhyme.]
I. Title.
PZ8.3.C96Ab   1993                              92-9621
[E]—dc20                                            CIP
                                                           AC

For Nancy, who loves a good mystery

**A** is the **A**rt that was stolen at night.

B is the **B**utler, who sneaks out of sight.

**C** is the **C**lue that's left in the room.

**D** is **D**etective Inspector McGroom.

**E** is the **E**ye that looks through the glass.

**F** is the **F**ootprint that's found in the grass.

**G** is the **G**ardener, who saw nothing that day.

**H** is his **H**elper, who has nothing to say.

**I** is **I**nspector, who ponders the case.

J is Jalopy, in which they give chase.

**K** is the **K**ilt that the bagpiper wore.

**L** is the **L**ake with a boat on the shore.

**M** is the **M**anor that stands on the moor.

**N** is the **N**umber of steps to the door.

**O** is the **O**rgan that sounds in the hall.

**P** is the **P**ainting with eyes that see all.

**Q** is the **Q**uery Dame Agatha makes.

**R** is the **R**obber, who's seen by mistake.

**S** is the **S**tairs to the cellar below.

**T** is the **Tunnel** through which they must go.

**U** is **U**mbrella that pries the door wide.

**V** is the **V**ault with the artwork inside.

**W** is **W**ombat and a den full of thieves.

**X** is the kiss the Inspector receives.

**Y** is a **Y**awn with the red setting sun.

**Z** is asleep . . . and a job that's well done.